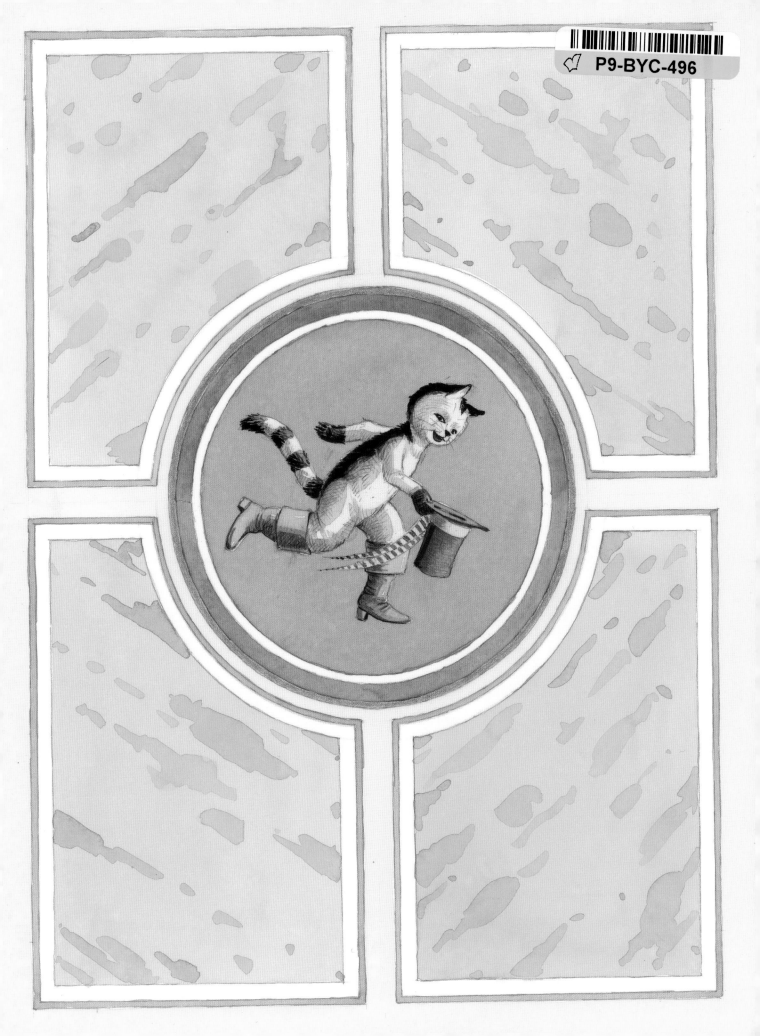

THE CLASSIC
FAIRY TALE COLLECTION

Puss in Boots

Retold by **JOHN CECH**

Illustrated by **BERNHARD OBERDIECK**

STERLING

New York / London

THERE WAS ONCE a miller who was so poor that, when he died, all he was able to leave his son was a cat. It was a nice cat, with fine whiskers and a big bushy tail, but still, it was just a cat.

"My poor father," the young man said. "A life of backbreaking work and all he had left was this cat."

"Cheer up," said the cat. "It could be worse."

"How could it *possibly* be worse?" the young man asked, not in the least bit surprised that the cat could talk. "I don't have a penny to my name, and no one would buy *you* at the market."

"Oh, I wouldn't sell me if I were you," the cat said. "I can change your fortunes. You'll see."

"If that's so, why didn't you change my father's fortunes?" asked the young man.

"All he ever wanted me to do was chase the rats out of the mill," answered the cat.

The young man thought awhile and said, "Well, *anything* is worth a try at this point."

"Exactly," said the cat. "Now, if you would, please bring me a pair of boots, a hat with a feather, and a cloth bag." Then he curled up and purred himself to sleep. While the cat was dozing, the young man borrowed a pair of high boots from one neighbor, a hat with a feather from another, and a sack with a drawstring from a third. When he returned, the cat was just getting up from his nap.

"Ah," said the cat. "That is all I need."

The cat put on his boots and hat and was gone. How he managed to slide into the boots and walk in them is anyone's guess. But talking cats can often surprise you.

Puss in his boots soon came upon some fishermen. When they weren't looking, he helped himself to the biggest fish in their nets. He tucked it, still wriggling, into his sack, then threw the sack over his shoulder and headed for the castle, where he presented the magnificent fish to the king.

"Will Your Majesty please accept this small token of deep respect, with the compliments of my master, Lord Fortunato?" Puss said with a flourish of his hat.

The next day, Puss brought the king a sack of juicy apples. The day after, Puss poured out a flood of chestnuts for His Majesty. A day later, he brought ripe sweet corn, and the day after that he filled the sack with the rarest mushrooms in the land. And thus it went every day for the next month—singing birds, strawberries, oysters, tender potatoes, crusty loaves of fresh bread, and tarts so sweet they made you smile. Where Puss found all of these things, no one knew.

Each time he presented a gift, Puss removed his hat with great dignity, bowed, and announced, "For Your Majesty's pleasure, with the compliments of my master, Lord Fortunato."

"I must meet your master," the king told Puss when the cat brought him a sack of succulent cherries, which the king and queen quickly ate with delight.

"So it shall be," the cat replied. "My master will be honored."

"Honored!?" the young man exclaimed when Puss told him about meeting the king. "How can I go to the palace in the rags that I'm wearing? And what would I say to the king?"

"Just do exactly as I say, and leave the rest to me," replied the cat as he kicked off his boots, curled up into a ball, and went instantly to sleep.

The next day, the king awoke to cries of alarm from the river that flowed past his castle.

"Help! Help! Lord Fortunato is drowning!"

The king and his guards raced to the riverbank and pulled the young man out of the water. He was soaked and breathless. His clothing was in tatters.

"My master was on his way to the castle," Puss announced, "with a gift of gold and jewels, to pay his respects to Your Majesty. But robbers attacked us and stole everything. They tore my master's clothes and threw him into the river. Why, I barely escaped with my whiskers and boots!"

"You poor lad," said the king. "And you poor cat! We'll soon have you dried off."

The king could not do enough for the young man. He took him to the castle, gave him a suit of his own clothes to wear, and fed him a hearty lunch.

"I'm sorry we don't have any more cherries," the king said. "They were the best that I have ever eaten. Wherever did you find them?"

The young man didn't know what to say, but before the king could notice the bewildered look on his face, the cat interrupted.

"Your Majesty, my master's country is rich and plentiful," Puss boasted. "The cherries are just a small sample of the rare treats to be found there."

"I must visit your country," the king announced. "With all the work of being king, I don't travel very much. Perhaps you can accompany us and show us your lands once you have rested up."

"Of course," Puss replied. "My master would be very happy to do just that." The young man nodded eagerly, thinking, *What has that cat gotten me into now?*

The king had his reasons for wanting to see where the young man had come from. He had only one daughter and was looking for a suitable young man who might be worthy of her hand in marriage. Naturally, the king was cautious. *I can't let just anyone who floats down the river marry the princess*, he thought.

The princess and the young man met that night at dinner, and they talked together all evening long.

"Hmmmm," the king said to the queen. "This is promising."

The next day, the princess and the young man went riding on horseback over the hills. They had a splendid time and came back laughing and singing together.

"Now this is *really* promising," said the queen to the king.

And so the king and the queen decided to go visit the young man's home. But when they announced this, the young man's face turned pale.

"My master would be honored to have you as his guests," Puss immediately offered. "Nothing would please him more!"

"Nothing would please me more!?" the young man exclaimed when he and the cat were alone that evening. "I'll be lucky if I keep my head on my shoulders when the king finds out who I really am."

"I've gotten you this far, haven't I?" Puss asked him. "Just leave it all to me." And with that the cat curled up on his silken bed and was soon in a deep, purring sleep.

The young man stayed up all night worrying.

In the morning, the castle began to bustle. Grooms saddled horses, footmen readied the coach, and maids and butlers packed food and clothing for travel into a wagon.

"I shall go on ahead and make sure that everything is ready for Your Majesties," Puss told the king, queen, and princess. "Take your time and enjoy the fine weather and the beautiful scenery as you go. Just travel west, and all will be waiting for your arrival."

Puss and his master hurried ahead along the road. "Just keep out of sight and let me do all the talking," Puss said to the young man. On his rambles, Puss had learned the road well, and he knew that he could turn it into a road of good fortune for his master.

When he left the king's country, he saw a group of farmers at work in one of the fields.

"Whose land is this?" Puss asked one of them.

"These are the fields of a horrible ogre," said a farmer, mopping his brow. "If we don't finish our work, we'll be out of much more than a job—you know what I mean?"

"The ogre can change himself into anything," another farmer added. "You never know when he's going to turn up or what he's going to be."

Puss replied, "Later today, a king and his company will come down this very road. The king seems like a kind fellow, but he's even meaner than the ogre. You don't want to cross him. If he's not happy, there's no telling what he might do! When he asks whose lands these are, be sure to say exactly this: 'They belong to Lord Fortunato.' Since Lord Fortunato is one of the king's favorite noblemen, it will please His Majesty to hear this."

When the king's party arrived a while later, the king asked the farmers whose land they were harvesting.

"It belongs to Lord Fortunato," the farmers replied, exactly as Puss had told them to do.

And so they went down the road, past orchards and berry patches, ponds and villages. Puss had been there first, and when the king asked who owned the rich countryside, the reply was always, "Lord Fortunato."

Puss and the young man reached the ogre's castle long before the others. While the young man hid behind some nearby bushes, Puss knocked at the large oak door and the ogre himself answered. He had just finished his lunch and was feeling chatty.

"Well, cat, what brings you here?" the ogre asked.

"Sir, I was just passing through and was curious to know if the stories were true," Puss said. "You know how curious cats are."

"What stories?" asked the ogre.

"Well, sir . . . I . . . what I've been hearing is that among your many powers, you can change yourself into anything you'd like."

"That's true, cat. And since you're the first cat I've ever seen wearing boots and a hat, I'll humor you," replied the ogre. "What would you like me to become?"

"I don't suppose you can become an elephant. That might be asking too much."

"Oh, not at all," replied the ogre. "It's very simple. Just watch!"

The ogre spun around three times in the entry hall, making a great cloud of smoke. When the smoke lifted, there, before Puss's wide eyes, stood an enormous elephant, trumpeting loudly through its trunk.

"That is truly astonishing," said Puss. "But is it also possible for someone as . . . well . . . *monumental* as yourself to become something very small?"

"Why, yes, of course it is," said the ogre after he had spun himself back into his former self. "What would you like to see me change into next?"

"Well, I'm sure it's quite beneath your dignity and your powers," said Puss, "but can you turn yourself into a mouse?"

"Just watch," said the ogre. Once again, he spun around three times. In a puff of smoke, he became a little mouse with a long tail and whiskers.

"My, that's some trick," said Puss, and he quickly snatched the mouse. He put it into his sack and tied the sack so close to the bottom that the ogre-turned-mouse couldn't spin around in it.

Just then, the king's coach arrived in the ogre's courtyard.

"I'll find a place for you later," Puss said to the sack, tucking it out of sight behind the bushes where the young man had been hiding. He pulled his master from behind the shrubs just in time to meet their guests.

"Your Majesty," the cat said, greeting the king. "Welcome to my lord's humble castle."

The king, queen, and princess were impressed by everything they had seen on their journey, but they liked the castle most of all, with its large halls, beautiful, soaring windows, and lovely gardens. Whatever one might say about the ogre, he had excellent taste.

"This is just the place for a wedding," the king announced as he placed his daughter's hand into that of the young man. And so the two were married that very day, and lived long and happy lives together in the castle. The people of the ogre's country loved their kind and generous new princess and Lord Fortunato. And they loved Puss, too, the cat in boots who had rid them of the ogre.

And the ogre? All his constant wriggling inside the bag made his magic wear off. When Puss finally let him out, he could only chase his tail round and round until he finally gave up. He still lives inside the walls of the castle, and Puss never forgets to leave him some cheese.

About the Story

The story of the clever cat that improves the fortunes of its poor owner is hundreds of years old. In fact, this tricky creature purrs along quite nicely in an Italian tale from the 1500s called "Constantino Fortunato," which appears in a collection by Giovanni Francesco Straparola entitled *Le piacevoli notti* (*The Pleasant Nights*). Many scholars of fairy tales believe that Straparola borrowed the story from one that had long been in circulation in the oral tradition of Italian folklore, but they also think that his is the earliest printed version of this tale. Another Italian author, Giambattista Basile, later included a version of this story (which he titled "Gagliuso") in his well-known collection, *Il Pentamerone* (circa 1634). In Basile's retelling, the cat is female. After she has successfully married off her master, Gagliuso, to the king's daughter and brought him great fortune, she gives him one final test. The cat wishes to see if her master will honor his promise to give her a regal burial when she dies, which she pretends to do. Gagliuso fails miserably, showing callous indifference to her feigned death, and although the cat doesn't punish him, she disappears, never to be seen again.

Perhaps the most familiar version of the fairy tale appeared in the fabled collection *Stories or Tales from Times Past; or, Tales of Mother Goose* (1697), by the French writer Charles Perrault. Perrault called his story "The Master Cat; or Puss in Boots" and made it part of his small volume of tales that was attributed to that most famous of all storytellers, Mother Goose, whose name in France was synonymous with the generic grandmotherly teller of tales. The volume also included some of the earliest versions of such fairy tales as "Little Red Riding Hood" and "Cinderella."

Although Perrault believed the vast majority of children are quite able to tell the difference between the kind of fantastical conduct allowed in a story and the behavior that is permitted in reality, the celebration of resourceful trickery in his story was not always appreciated by critics of his fairy tales. But this criticism has done little to lessen the popularity of "Puss in Boots," and other stories like it, among children. After all, what reader doesn't want to imagine a clever animal rescuing him or her from misfortune—like the gazelle does in the African tale called "The Gazelle," which closely resembles "Puss in Boots" in many ways, or like the wise and wonderful cats that appear in trickster tales from Russia and Norway to Greece and Sicily? In England, people still tell the tale of Dick Whittington, a poor boy who uses his only penny to buy a cat that brings him such a fortune, he becomes the mayor of London.

Whether large or small, cats are often regarded as nocturnal animals, and so have been associated for centuries with "the dark side." But it should be remembered that cats were revered in ancient Egypt and later by the Prophet Mohammed. According to one biblical legend, cats also played an essential role on Noah's Ark—they kept it from being overrun by mice. And in Japan, cats are often thought of as lucky. Small statues of cats are even placed at the entrances of shops to invite good fortune inside. After all, according to folklore, cats lead charmed lives—all nine of them!

—J. C.

FOR SUZIE AND TING-A-LING and, of course, for Nedjem,
that fabled first cat, the sweetest of all.   –J. C.

STERLING and the distinctive Sterling logo are registered trademarks of
Sterling Publishing Co., Inc.

Library of Congress Cataloging-in-Publication Data

Cech, John.
Puss in boots / retold by John Cech ; illustrated by Bernhard Oberdieck.
p. cm. -- (The classic fairy tale collection)
Summary: A clever cat helps his poor master win fame, fortune, and the hand of a beautiful princess.
Includes historical notes on versions of this tale and other fairy tales.
ISBN 978-1-4027-4436-5
[1. Fairy tales. 2. Folklore--France.] I. Oberdieck, Bernhard, ill. II. Puss in boots. English III. Title.
PZ8.C293Pu 2010
398.2--dc22
[E]
2008052496

Lot#:
2 4 6 8 10 9 7 5 3 1
11/09
Published by Sterling Publishing Co., Inc.
387 Park Avenue South, New York, NY 10016
Text © 2010 by John Cech
Illustrations © 2010 by Bernhard Oberdieck
The illustrations in this book were created using watercolor, pen, and ink.
Distributed in Canada by Sterling Publishing
c/o Canadian Manda Group, 165 Dufferin Street
Toronto, Ontario, Canada M6K 3H6
Distributed in the United Kingdom by GMC Distribution Services
Castle Place, 166 High Street, Lewes, East Sussex, England BN7 1XU
Distributed in Australia by Capricorn Link (Australia) Pty. Ltd.
P.O. Box 704, Windsor, NSW 2756, Australia

Printed in China

Sterling ISBN 978-1-4027-4436-5

For information about custom editions, special sales, premium and
corporate purchases, please contact Sterling Special Sales
Department at 800-805-5489 or specialsales@sterlingpublishing.com.

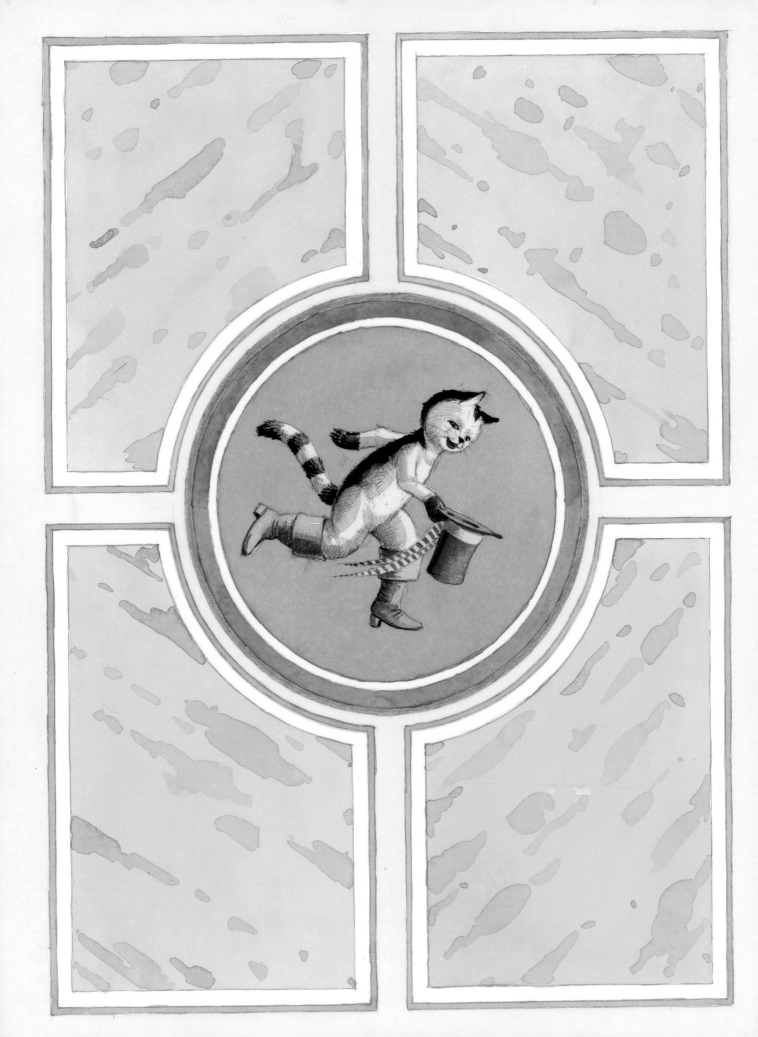